This book belongs to:

Emily von Gunten

From

Mom Mom   1992

Witch stories

Illustrated by
JANE LAUNCHBURY

DERRYDALE BOOKS
New York

Printed and bound in Malaysia

ISBN 0-517-06526-6

87654321

CONTENTS

EDWARD AND ANNA 8

THE MAGIC ISLAND 16

WITCH WURZEL 23

THE WITCHES WHO
  CAME TO STAY 31

GRUMBLOG 39

THE WITCH WHO
  DIDN'T HAVE A CAT 46

RACHEL AND THE
  MAGIC STONE 53

EDWARD AND ANNA

by Jane Launchbury

F ar away, at the edge of a great mountain range, there lived a poor woman and her two children, a boy called Edward, and a girl called Anna. Two winters ago, their loving father had set off to hunt deer in the mountains, but there had been a terrible avalanche and he had never returned. Every night the children lit a lamp in the tiny cottage window, in the hope that it would guide him home; but all that ever came were big furry moths, spinning dizzily towards the light.

One dark night there was a terrible storm in the mountains. Lightning flashed across the sky, thunder crashed, and echoes rumbled down the valleys. Edward and Anna rushed into their mother's room and huddled against her in bed. Outside, the rain lashed against the

windows, and the wild wind howled angrily through the trees and down the chimney. The lamp at the cottage window flared and flickered, sending eerie shadows dancing over the walls, but it didn't go out.

"Don't worry," said the children's mother, cuddling them to her, "it's only a horrid old storm. It'll soon go away."

But the storm got worse and worse. Suddenly, a great thunder crash was followed by a terrible creaking and screaming, as though a vast monster was heading straight for them. The old chestnut tree behind the cottage was tearing its roots from the ground. It seemed to fall in slow motion on to the little cottage. There was a horrible sound as roof timbers smashed. Tiles flew in all direction. Twigs, tiles and rain poured in through a gaping hole. The children and their mother took refuge in the old woodshed. At least it was dry in there. All night the storm raged, but at the cottage window the lamp burned steadily on.

When daylight came, and the last rumbles of thunder had vanished over the mountains, the family crept out of the woodshed. They looked gloomily at their home. There was very little left of the roof. Sadly, they walked around the soggy rooms, looking up at the brightening sky through the gaping hole.

"Whatever are we going to do?" sighed Anna. She knew that they could not afford a new roof. Then she had an idea. Once she had gone up into the mountains with her father to gather reeds from beside a great blue lake. "I know," she gasped. "We can cut reeds and thatch the roof ourselves."

So, as soon as the sun had fully risen, the children's mother gave them a bag with the last small scraps of bread and cheese. She told them to keep to the paths and hurry back home before dark. Then she waved goodbye and Edward and Anna set off for the lake in the mountains.

For hours the children walked up winding paths that lead higher and higher into the mountains. At last they saw the great blue lake, shimmering in a valley below them and they ran cheerfully towards it.

Around the edges of the lake grew the tall reeds that Anna had remembered. The reeds grew most thickly in a dark inlet, shadowed by a mountain crag. Edward and Anna settled down to work there straight away. It was much quicker than cutting the reeds that grew in the sunshine, but there was a chilly feel to the place. Soon they became aware of another sound above the croaking of the mountain frogs which were all around them. It sounded like a wheezy voice whispering something. Edward and Anna stopped work and looked around.

They couldn't see anyone. Then they heard the voice again. This time it was much clearer.

"Swish, swosh, who DARES to take,
Reeds that grow in MY lake?"

A bony old woman crept out of the shadows. She was the ugliest person they had ever seen. She was bent over a stick and, as she hobbled closer, the children saw that her skin was a sort of greenish yellow.

Anna and Edward backed away, but there was no escape. Behind them, there was only the tangled reed bed and the deep blue lake. Around them, the mountain frogs had begun to croak in unison. They seemed to be saying something: "Beware of the Witch of the Lake," they croaked over and over again.

Then the old woman spoke, in quite a friendly voice.

"You must be hungry my little chickens. Come into my house and I'll give you a nice meal. Then you'll be strong enough to cut as many reeds as you need."

Edward and Anna were a little comforted by this, but still they didn't move.

"Come along my little froglets," she said, edging towards them.

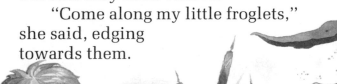

This time they didn't have any choice. Taking them by the hands, the old woman led the two children into her house. Outside, the frogs croaked louder than ever.

"Here, child. Help me light the fire," she crooned to Anna. "Then I can cook you a real feast. You, boy. Go and fetch fresh water from the well outside and fill this pot," she said, pointing a crooked finger at a vast cauldron. "Hurry now."

Edward went gloomily out to the well. He did not trust the old woman, but he couldn't just run off and leave his sister. He leaned over the well and sighed heavily. It was a very deep well, and his sigh echoed around and around its depths. Then he heard another sound.

On a ledge just inside the well shaft, there sat a handsome green frog with shiny yellow eyes. Drops of water glittered on its back, like jewels. It looked up at Edward and spoke:

"The old woman is a wicked witch. She is going to eat you up. You must trick her and escape."

"Oh no!" gasped Edward. "How can I trick her?" Then he had an idea. "How deep is the well?" he asked.

"Deeper than the night," replied the frog, pushing a little pebble down the shaft. Edward waited to hear the splash as it hit the water. When it eventually came, the sound was so faint that he could only just hear it.

"Stay there kind frog. Keep croaking as loudly as you can," he said. Then he ran back to the witch's house.

"Come outside," called Edward. "There's a huge fat frog in the well. It would make a delicious meal." The old witch needed no further bidding, and she lurched over to the well. Anna ran after her. The little frog was hiding in a crack, and croaking with all its might.

The old witch peered into the depths of the well, but she couldn't see any huge, fat frogs.

"It's down there," said Edward, pointing into the darkness. "Can't you see it?" The old woman leaned even further into the well, licking her lips.

"Now!" shouted Edward. "Push!" He and Anna gave the witch a great shove.

The witch let out a shriek and toppled over into the well. Down, down, she tumbled. Edward listened for the splash. At last it came. The echoes lasted for quite a while, then all was quiet. The wicked witch had gone forever. Then, out of the gloom, they heard the croaking of the frog. Edward leaned into the well, and lifted the little creature out in his hands.

"Thank you, frog," he whispered. Then he kissed it gently on the top of its head.

There was a blinding flash, and the little frog turned into a tall man.

"Anna! Edward!" he cried.

"Father!" gasped the children, rushing into his arms. "We thought you had been swept away forever in the avalanche," said Anna.

"No," said their father. "The wicked witch caught

me. She turned me into a frog for her supper, but I escaped and I've been living here in the well ever since. You must have broken the spell." Then the children told their father about the great storm, that had destroyed their roof, and how they had come to gather reeds by the lake. "Oh my clever, brave children!" cried their father. "We must collect the reeds and get home to your mother as fast as we can."

It was nearly dark as they set off down the stony paths. As the sky got darker, a tiny glow from the foot of the mountain got stonger. The children's mother had lit the lamp in the cottage window, and its light drew them all back to home and safety at last.

THE END

THE MAGIC ISLAND

by Elizabeth Waugh

Far, far away, in the warm South Seas, there is a magic island, ruled over by a kindly witch called Thomasina Toffee. On Thomasina's island the sea shells are made of bubblegum, the streams flow with sparkling lemonade and huge chocolate buttons grow on the trees. For Thomasina had a sweet tooth, and there was nothing she liked better than to nibble a tasty little sweet. As she was a witch, and her teeth were made of good strong crystal, she never needed any fillings, and could eat as many sweets as she liked. Thomasina's broomstick was made of barley sugar, and every day she would ride on it around her island, flying high over the cream soda waterfalls and the toffee trees.

One night, when Thomasina was fast asleep in her marzipan bed, she was woken suddenly by the sound of

the wind howling and the waves crashing on the shore.
There was a terrible storm. The wind was blowing so
hard that the chocolate buttons were pitter-pattering
down from the trees, and the pear drop sea shells were
being whirled along the beach.

Crossly, Thomasina got out of bed, put on her magic
spangled cloak and made her way down to the beach.
She tried to make a spell to calm the storm, but her
magic was not strong enough. In the distance she could
see a ship rolling and heaving on the waves. She was a
good witch and would liked to have helped, but there
was nothing she could do. So she went back to her little
toffee house, shut the door firmly, and got into bed.

When she woke in the morning, the sun was
shining and the sea was calm and still. She was drinking
her breakfast cup of hot chocolate when suddenly she
heard a loud:

"ACHOOO!"

It came from the beach. But who could it be?
Nobody else lived on Thomasina's island.
She quickly jumped
on her barley sugar
broomstick and flew
down to the sea-
shore. There,
sitting on a rock
and looking very
cold, wet and
bedraggled,
was a little
yellow
teddy bear.

17

"Achooo!" he sneezed and spluttered and shivered. Thomasina floated down beside him.

"Zimblebee-fiddle-me-dee!" she said. "And who are you?"

"My name is – ACHOOO! – Ernest Pumpkin," said the little teddy bear. "I was sailing with my family on a big ship, and I got washed overboard in a terrible storm."

"Well, my dear Mr Pumpkin," said Thomasina, kindly. "Welcome to my magic island! You must come back to my house to dry yourself!"

"Please call me Ernest," said the teddy bear. "Thank you for your kind invitation. I should very much like to dry myself. ACHOOO!"

So Ernest climbed on the back of Thomasina's broomstick, and back they flew to her little toffee house.

The sun was shining, and Ernest soon dried off. Thomasina offered him all sorts of delicious things to eat: a thimble-full of raspberryade, a slice of fudge, a little plate of chocolate buttons. Then she took him on a lovely ride around the island, and showed him the cream soda waterfall and the pear drop sea shells. That evening Thomasina gave him his own little bed and Ernest slept better than ever before.

Ernest loved sweets too, so he had a wonderful time on Thomasina's magic island. He stayed for several weeks, steadily growing fatter and fatter. But one day Thomasina noticed that he was looking very sad. He hadn't bothered to eat his breakfast, and he was sitting gloomily on the doughnut sofa staring ahead of him. Then a fat tear rolled down his cheek and plopped onto the floor.

"Whatever is the matter, Ernest?" asked Thomasina, anxiously.

"I miss my family," said Ernest, sadly, "and especially Jennifer, the little girl who owned me. I wonder where she is now? She must miss me too!"

"Well, let's have a look in my crystal ball," said Thomasina. "Then we can see what they are all doing."

Thomasina brought a beautiful, shining, round object out of her cupboard. "It's magic," she explained. "If you look into it, you can see where your friends are and what they are doing."

Thomasina placed it carefully on the table and said her magic spell:

> "Crystal ball, shining bright,
> Through the day and through the night,
> Tell me where is Jennifer now?"

As they peered into the crystal ball, shapes slowly began to form. "Why, look!" cried Ernest. "It's Jennifer! And her mother! They're in a house by the seaside!"

"Well, that's easy!" said Thomasina. "I can take you there on my broomstick. But we will have to go at night, so that nobody sees us. And we had better wear my spangled cloak, in case it gets cold."

So, that very night, Thomasina and Ernest set off on the barley sugar broomstick. They whizzed through the moonlight, over islands and oceans, until they came to the house where Ernest's family was staying. They floated down on the broomstick and landed in the garden. As quietly as a little mouse, Thomasina opened the back door by magic, and Ernest tiptoed into the sitting room and jumped onto the sofa. He kissed Thomasina goodbye, and thanked her very much for her kindness. Then she climbed back onto the broomstick and flew back home to her magic island.

When Jennifer came down for breakfast the following morning, she was amazed to see Ernest sitting on the sofa. She rushed up to him, and hugged and kissed him.

"Mummy! Mummy!" she yelled. "Guess what! Ernest has come back! Come and see!"

And so Ernest returned to live happily with his family. But as he sat in the nursery with the other toys, eagerly waiting for Jennifer to bring some crumpets for tea, he often thought of the kindly witch Thomasina and her magic island, where all those good things to eat could be had if you just stretched out your paw.

And, as for Jennifer, she never understood why Ernest had grown so fat...

THE END

WITCH WURZEL

by Elizabeth Waugh

Witch Wurzel lived in a dark, smelly cave on Bald Mountain. Her cat, Snout, helped her with her spells, but he was simply not good enough. Snout would nibble the magic mushrooms on the sly and spill the crab apple juice. He was also very bad at catching earwigs. Witch Wurzel needed an apprentice to prepare her spells properly. So, one morning, she set off in search of a child to help her.

At the foot of Bald Mountain there was a cottage where two cousins, Nicholas and Sarah, lived. They never went into the dark pine woods on the slopes of Bald Mountain, because of the bats that flitted about there and the owls that screeched.

This afternoon they were sitting by the well playing with Pattypaws, Nicholas's kitten. Nicholas always fed Pattypaws on special scraps he saved from his meals, and she followed him everywhere.

23

Witch Wurzel crept up to the hedge that grew around the well and peeped over the top.

"These children look a suitable size," she thought. "One of them will do nicely as an apprentice." Just then, Sarah's mother called her.

The girl reluctantly left her cousin playing with Pattypaws and went to join her mother. Witch Wurzel flicked hastily through her alphabetical book of magic to find the spell she wanted: "Fungus ... Frogspawn ... Aha, here we are, Forgetfulness."

She crawled out from behind the hedge and glared at Nicholas, who froze in terror.

Fumbling in her pockets, she brought out the magic ingredients and threw them at Nicholas's feet. Then she chanted the spell:

> *"Adder's bite and dead dog's bone,*
> *Forget all you have ever known,*
> *Aunties, uncles, cousins too,*
> *And do what I shall ask of you."*

Pattypaws had scurried into the bushes. Nicholas's face went blank and he stared helplessly at Witch Wurzel.

"That should do very well," she cackled gleefully. "Now follow me, child," and Nicholas did just that.

When Sarah returned she found Pattypaws mewing sadly, and there was no sign of Nicholas at all. She searched in the orchard and down by the river, but he was nowhere to be found. That night all the villagers went in seach of him, but not a trace could be found. And they were all too frightened of witches to look in the woods on Bald Mountain.

Meanwhile, Witch Wurzel was delighted with her new servant. Silent and obedient, he mixed her glasses of nasty toadslime, he diced the fungus and cleaned the filthy cauldron, all at her command. Snout was no longer needed, and he sulked by the broomsticks. Nicholas never asked about his home, because he had forgotten that he ever had one.

All day he worked making spells, and at night he slept by the glowing cauldron.

Sarah's mother and the villagers decided that Nicholas would never return. Perhaps he had been swept away by the river and drowned. But Sarah felt sure that he was still alive somewhere. One day she was out walking, when a big black crow landed on a branch above her.

"Big black crow," sighed Sarah. "Can you tell me where my cousin is?" To her amazement, the crow opened his big beak and spoke:

"In Wild Witch Wurzel's gloomy caves,
Your cousin Nicholas toils and slaves.
Follow the path up the mountain side,
And there you will find where the Wild Witch hides!"

Sarah started forward to ask the crow more questions, but he had already flapped away. So she made her way back to the cottages, and resolved that she would go in search of her cousin. The next morning she set off along the winding path which led through the pine trees and up to the top of Bald Mountain.

Witch Wurzel was in a very good mood that morning. Nicholas and Snout had mixed her a revolting spotty potion, which she was going to sprinkle on the village teacher. She was sitting outside her cave, picking her teeth with a bat's claw, when she caught sight of Sarah coming up the mountain side.

"Aha!" she cried. "That silly girl. Come to fetch her cousin, no doubt. Well, my forgetfulness spell has lasted good and strong. He'll never recognise her."

Sarah shivered when she caught sight of the huge cauldron and the sinister figure of Witch Wurzel.

Then Witch Wurzel called out to her.

"Step this way, child. After your cousin, aren't you? Well, you'll soon see how strong my magic is."

Sarah stepped nervously forward. Just at that moment, Nicholas came out of the cave carrying a huge bundle of firewood for the cauldron.

"Nicholas!" cried Sarah, and ran forward to hug him. But Nicholas stared at her blankly, as though he had never seen her before. Witch Wurzel cackled in delight.

"He can't remember a thing!" she crowed. "See how strong my magic is!"

"I'll make him remember," said Sarah bravely. "I'll find a way."

Witch Wurzel was enjoying herself. She decided to play a game with this cheeky child – a game the girl would be sure to lose.

"Very well," she sneered. "Just see if you can make him remember. If you can, you can have him. But you will not succeed."

Sarah went over to her cousin, who was working inside the cave. He was busy stirring the witch's steaming cauldron, cooking up another horrid-smelling spell. He didn't even look up when Sarah went over and laid her hand gently on his arm.

"Nicholas," she said desperately. "You must remember our cottage and the hens in the back yard." But Nicholas just glanced at her and went back to his work. Witch Wurzel roared with laughter. This was good fun! Sarah tried again.

"Remember the wooden squirrel you carved that hangs by your bed," she said. "And the grandfather clock that doesn't work." But still Nicholas just looked at her as though he did not understand. Witch Wurzel cackled in delight.

Then suddenly, there was a loud mewing. Sarah looked down in astonishment to see Pattypaws racing towards Nicholas. The kitten must have followed her all the way up the mountain! Instantly Nicholas stopped looking blank. He knelt down and picked up Pattypaws, who purred and licked his face. Then he jumped up and hugged his cousin. "Sarah!" he cried happily.

Witch Wurzel flew into a furious rage. She scowled and shrieked and tried to bundle Nicholas back into her cave. But Sarah stepped between them.

"You promised to let him go if he remembered," she cried. "Your spell has worn off! You promised!"

Witch Wurzel could not break her promise. She spluttered with anger as Sarah led her cousin and Pattypaws away down Bald Mountain and back home, but she could do nothing. When the villagers heard that a little kitten had managed to break one of the witch's wicked spells, they all stopped being afraid of her. As for Witch Wurzel, she was so ashamed that she flew away and was never seen again.

THE END

The Witches
who
Came to Stay

by Philip Steele

Once upon a time there were three wicked witches, who went to sea in a ship full of holes. The ship's mast was an upturned broomstick and, instead of a flag, there were tattered streamers of seaweed. As soon as the ship set sail, the sky turned yellow and filled with big black clouds. A storm came whirling across the bay, tossing the spray up into the wind. But the ship sped on and on, scudding over the waves like a cormorant. And if you had listened carefully above the howling wind, you might have heard the wicked witches singing to themselves:

> *"Sea snakes and jelly fish,*
> *Octopi and smelly fish,*
> *Skellingtons in wellingtons*
> *Forty fathoms deep!"*

The wicked witches cackled with glee, and then peered through their telescopes.

"Land ahoy! Land ahoy!"

The ship sped on and on, towards a little island on the horizon...

Granite Island was a lonely place, especially during an autumn storm. Fergus the Fisherman pulled his boat high up on the beach, and went home to his little stone cottage.

"What an evening!" he said to himself, as he barred the door behind him. "Why, it must be nearly Hallowe'en!" He put a big kettle on the fire, and pulled off his boots. Outside, the storm was raging. Waves were crashing against the sea wall. Fergus could hear them: Crash! Splash! Splosh!
It was at times like this that he wished he didn't live all on his own.

Just then, Fergus heard a knock on the door. Or was it simply a loose plank banging in the wind? Was that rain spattering on the window pane? Or maybe the scrabble of long finger nails? And was that the sound of the wind, or someone singing?

> "Skellingtons in wellingtons
> Forty fathoms deep!..."

Fergus shivered. Then he strode across to the door and flung it open. In tumbled a bedraggled brood of witches, who fell on the floor in a heap!

"Who the devil are you?" thundered Fergus.

A thin witch with knobbly knees untangled herself. She pulled on her tall black hat, which was dripping wet.

"I am Bignose, a wicked witch," said she, "and I can turn you into a sea slug — just like that!" She snapped her bony fingers.

A big fat witch with fifteen double chins was the next to get up on her feet. She carried a large carpetbag.

"I am Fishface, an even wickeder witch!" said she, "and I can turn you into an archaeopteryx!"

Fergus didn't know what an archaeowhatsit was, but he didn't like the sound of it at all. Still, he put a brave face on it. He pulled up the third witch by her scarlet shawl.

"And which witch are you?" he demanded.

"Which witch? *Which witch*? Are you *mocking* me?" The third witch turned towards him, and she had the most beautiful face Fergus had ever seen. Her long red hair was a tangle of curls, and her eyes were as blue as the summer sea. "Because if you *are* mocking me," she went on, "I shall turn you into driftwood and burn you on the fire! My name is Belladonna, and I have come to stay here for Hallowe'en, with my aunties Fishface and Bignose!"

"Oh, you have, have you? And who invited you?" Fergus was furious, but all three witches stared at him sternly, and he had no desire to be frizzled and fried, or turned into some creepy-crawly. "All right, all right," he added quickly. "You can stay. But only for Hallowe'en mind you..."

"Agreed," snapped Bignose. "Now, we three are very tired, so we'll be off to bed."

"And in the meantime I suggest you prepare our breakfast for tomorrow," added Fishface.

Fergus cursed his luck. Witches to stay! They'd cause all sorts of trouble. And where was he to sleep? Here in the chair? Fishface and Bignose indeed! Belladonna was very beautiful, it was true ...but wasn't

it she who wanted to make firewood out of him? What was Fergus to do?

The night passed by, and Fergus dozed fitfully by the fire. The wind was still moaning around the cottage. As the firelight flickered, Fergus caught sight of a book sticking out of Fishface's carpetbag. He carefully pulled it out and looked at the cover. It was called *Every Witch's Handbook of Practical Spells*. He turned the pages with growing excitement.

After half an hour, Fergus pulled on his boots and slipped out of the front door. He returned around dawn, his pockets bulging with odds and ends which he emptied out on the table. There was a crab's claw and a dollop of tar, some clammy seaweed and a smelly old fish bone! What was he up to?

The next day the witches woke up to a delicious smell of cooking. Sunshine was pouring in through the door.

"Breakfast time, you wicked witches!" called Fergus. "Tasty pies to start the day!"

"Well, this *is* nice," said Bignose, and gobbled up her pie in two mouthfuls.

"Yum, yum," she said, smacking her lips greedily. "That was very tasty!"

"Maybe we won't turn you into a sea slug after all," croaked Fishface, and gobbled up hers.

"Not until after the holiday's over," explained Belladonna, and smiled icily as she bit into her pie.

Suddenly the witches looked a little pale. Bignose was growing a yellow beak, and squawking like a gull! Fishface was turning into a plump porpoise, before their very eyes!!

"Shoo! Shoo!" laughed Fergus. The gull flew out of the front door, and away over the sea. Fergus threw the porpoise over the sea wall, and away it swam. Belladonna was white with rage. She started muttering spells, but Fergus just stood there chuckling.

"What have you done, you oaf?" said Belladonna, stamping her foot.

"I have used your little book to make some magic potions," replied Fergus. "Now you can have a taste of your own medicine. Your wicked aunties have been turned into animals for a year and a day. That should teach them better manners!"

"But what about *me*?" wailed Belladonna.

"You have just swallowed a love potion, and will love me as long as you live!"

And so she had and so she did. In fact, Fergus and Belladonna were married the very next day. Fergus was never lonely again, and Belladonna and he were very much in love. Sometimes Belladonna still tried out new spells, but she never ever wanted to turn Fergus into firewood. And sometimes, when the autumn gales blew, they could see a little black boat with a broomstick mast bob over the horizon, and in the wind they could hear snatches of songs about skeletons under the sea. But Fishface and Bignose never came to stay again. They had learned their lesson well.

THE END

GRUMBLOG

by June Garrett

There was once a beautiful land which was terrorised by an evil witch. Her name was Grumblog and she could not bear anything that was peaceful, happy or beautiful. It made her boil over with rage. Her eyes would send out showers of red sparks and thick black smoke would pour from her ears. The people in the village near the forest where she lived were terrified. They thought a volcano was erupting.

Grumblog's forest was a dangerous place. People entering it in search of blackberries, or wild mushrooms, seldom reappeared. So, a ripple of fear spread through the village one morning when a really loud and dreadful volcano rage from Grumblog was followed by an eerie silence. All the birds stopped singing. Nothing moved, except the wind in the trees.

The witch had got extremely cross at the sight of a blackbird singing to a pair of courting squirrels. She hated anyone to be happy. Spitting with terrible rage, she stirred her cauldron savagely. Then, looking up at the cloud of evil-smelling steam, she hissed:

*"Fur and feather, be no more.
Turn to stone by Grumblog's lore."*

In that instant, the whole forest fell silent. The villagers were so scared, they packed up their things and fled across the hills.

In the forest, all the wild creatures had been turned into stone. Tiny statues of mice, rabbits and deer stood, with surprised looks on their faces, by the side of the path. When the sound of all the frightened people running away faded, all that could be heard was the wheezing of Grumblog, cackling over the success of her spell.

It did not take long, however, for Grumblog to discover that she had made a serious mistake. The forest was more beautiful than ever before. Flowers blossomed where the rabbits and deer used to graze. And everything was quiet and peaceful around the witch's dark and gloomy home, where she sat, thinking up new ways of making everyone miserable.

Grumblog flung down her book of spells in disgust.

"This is no good at all," she roared. "Bring me whirlwinds and thunderstorms, typhoons and tornados." And she kicked the sleeping cauldron with her boot.

But the storms she unleashed made the forest fresher, greener and lovelier than ever. And as she stumped through the deserted forest and the empty countryside, the cottage gardens with their bright flowers seemed to mock her. Grumblog went purple with rage. Black trails of smoke curled up over the treetops, as she marched back to her dark, damp home.

Plunging her broomstick into the cauldron, she stirred the magic brew as hard as she could, and cursed the flowers with the most fearful spell she knew:

"Cottage gardens, hedgerow weeds,
Live up to your names in deeds."

No one knows whether Grumblog actually intended the spell to work out the way it did, but immediately all the plants began to change.

Dandelions and tiger lilies turned into real lions and tigers, snarling crossly at each other. Elephant grasses grew greyer and fatter, until they became a herd of real elephants. The monkeypuzzle tree dissolved into a chattering colony of apes. Cows emerged from cowslips, and snapdragons grew into real dragons that set fire to the tree tops as they flapped overhead. Then all the plant-animals started chasing each other. The elephants stampeded through the cows, the lions and tigers fought the dragons — it was chaos! Grumblog was absolutely delighted.

The witch sat back and watched as the animals crashed through the wood, tearing up the grass, burning the leaves, and barking and snarling at each other. She roared with laughter as they fought, and croaked "Bravo!" as they knocked over bushes and fences, broke windows and generally made a terrible mess.

Then, Grumblog froze with fear, for she suddenly realised that the roar of the dandelions and the wild trumpeting of the elephant grasses were coming closer. The thudding of heavy feet and the crashing of branches got louder and louder – the plant-animals were heading straight for her!!

Grumblog dashed back to her hovel and managed to hide, just as a huge, angry herd of elephants, lions, tigers and dragons came smashing their way into her clearing, snapping her broomstick underfoot – and sending her precious magic cauldron flying.

From the moment that the evil-smelling liquid from the broken cauldron seeped into the ground, the forest began to change. Grumblog's wicked spell was broken! And not only that spell – but all the evil spells she had ever done. The stone birds and animals dotted about the forest came to life again, and carried on exactly as though nothing had happened. And the plant-animals changed back into their true form.

Suddenly, the villagers couldn't remember why they had left their beautiful valley. Filled with gladness, they packed their bags again for the journey home. But what they saw when they got there took their breath away. Their lovingly tended gardens lay in ruins and their favourite flowers were scattered across the countryside. It took them weeks to tidy up the mess.

As for Grumblog, no one ever discovered what became of her. Once her magic powers were destroyed, she vanished from the forest for ever, leaving the land in peace at last.

THE END

THE WITCH WHO DIDN'T HAVE A CAT

by Sue Seddon

There was once a witch called Smoragda who didn't have a cat. The Chief Witch wasn't very pleased about it, and commanded Smoragda to come and explain her lack of a cat in person. So Smoragda mounted her broomstick and flew to Castle Greydoom.

"Now look here, Smoragda," began the Chief Witch. "You must get yourself a cat. All witches have a cat. You can't be a witch without one."

"I don't want a cat," whined Smoragda.

"Stuff and nonsense! Why ever not?" snapped the Chief Witch.

Smoragda looked at her through her slanty green eyes and cracked her knobbly knuckles crossly.

"I don't like cats," she said.

"Not like cats! NOT LIKE CATS!" shrieked the

Chief Witch, her crumpled face quivering with rage.
"We'll see about that! I shall send you a cat tomorrow.
Do not try to get rid of it with spells. My magic is
stronger than yours. Now go home."

The next morning Smoragda was woken by a
dreadful, earsplitting yowl outside her window.

"The cat!" she thought, and went to the door.
Opening it, she saw a small, black cat sitting on the step.

"Scram!" yelled Smoragda, and slammed the door.
A few moments later she opened it again. The cat was
still there, with his back to her.

"Shoooooo!" hissed Smoragda.
The cat didn't even twitch his tail.
Then very slowly he turned his
head and fixed his great yellow
eyes on Smoragda and yawned.

"B-b-b-broomsticks and
buffaloes," growled
Smoragda, "this is going
to be difficult." And she
banged the door shut again.

All that day Smoragda worked her way through her *Giant Book of Spells*, especially the 'Disappearing', 'Vanishing' and 'Getting Rid Of' sections. But the spells were all useless. At bedtime the cat was still on the doorstep, though he had curled up and gone to sleep.

"Drat this cat," said Smoragda. "If magic doesn't work, I shall have to take him somewhere and lose him! Now, where shall I take him?"

In the morning Smoragda opened the door and called the cat:

"Pussy, Pussy, Pussy! Who's a nice little Pussy then? Come to mummy."

The cat opened an eye and uncurled itself slowly. It looked down its nose at the witch's shaggy red hair and long green fingernails, then arched its back and had a good stretch. Smoragda grabbed it. It let out a fearful yowl, but she hung on and galloped towards her broomstick. After a terrible fight, Smoragda managed to tie the cat onto the handle of the broomstick and, leaping astride, she took off.

High into the sky they flew, higher than a plane, and faster than a train. The air screamed past them and flattened the cat's ears to its head and its whiskers to its cheeks. Smoragda untied the cat:

"Hang on pussy cat," she cried, "or you might just fall off." And she let out a dreadful shriek of laughter.

Now Smoragda was famous for her aerobatics. She had won prizes for looping the loop, and her sky dives were spectacular. Roaring through the sky with the cat behind her,

she threw her broomstick into all the high-flying tricks she knew. She zig-zagged, she curled, she dodged and stalled. She went into a record head-dive which made even her own stomach turn over — but she couldn't shake the cat off. He sat calmly through it all.

At last, in desperation, she looped the biggest loop. It was so enormous that her heels hit the stars and made sparks fly. Everyone on Earth saw hundreds of shooting stars.

"This is it, cat. Say goodbye!" yelled Smoragda, as broomstick, witch and cat fell from the top of the loop into a death-defying dive. Even Smoragda was using all her magic to stay on. Her pointed witches' hat disappeared and so did the cat. Smoragda looked back to make quite sure and shouted a triumphant "Hooray!" But, when she turned round again, what a shock she got! For there was the cat, sitting on the front of the broomstick enjoying every minute of it. He had climbed round to get a better view.

So they shot down to Earth together and Smoragda tried everything she knew to make the cat fall off. She dived into the deepest ocean, but the cat loved the fish and asked her to do it again. She travelled through the hottest deserts, but the cat loved the sun. She tried to freeze him in Antarctica, but he got on very well with penguins. She even took him to the moon, but he said he'd always wanted to be the first cat to land there.

Exhausted, Smoragda returned home. The cat smiled and asked when they could go up again.

Smoragda went to see the Chief Witch.

"Okay, you win!" she said. "I'll keep the cat. I'm beginning to think he's rather special."

"He is," answered the Chief Witch. "I gave him nine lives."

So that is how Smoragda the witch got her cat.

THE END

RACHEL AND THE MAGIC STONE

by Deborah Tyler

Rachel Green lived in the middle of a row of three cottages at the end of Orchard Lane. Her parents' house was a pretty little cottage, but the other two were very strange indeed. They were very ugly and very squat. They had lots of rickety black chimney pots and they were covered with strange carvings. The carvings were of fierce beasts and they seemed to roar at passers-by. So you can see that the cottages were very strange indeed, and the reason they were so odd is because they belonged to two witches.

Rachel hated living there. It was no fun living between two old witches. Especially two old witches who were always arguing.

The two witches were sisters. Their names were Snatch and Grab and they were very mean. Snatch was

53

long and thin. She looked as if she was made out of sticks and joined together badly at the knees. She had a sharp nose, beady black eyes and no chin. She always wore purple lipstick and a pair of big emerald ear-rings. Sometimes, she wore an enormous hat, with flowers sticking out of it. It was really rather a funny hat, but no one dared to laugh at it.

Grab was as plain as her sister was colourful. Rachel always thought she looked as if she was made from a potato. She wore a grey jumper, a black skirt and thick, grey stockings, which always had huge holes in them. She had a fat, dimpled face and wild, wiry grey hair.

Long ago, the Great White Witch had given the two sisters a stone. It was a magic stone, made from unicorn's horn and dragon's wing, and it had very special powers. It could heal anything and it could also be used to cast spells.

In the summer, the magic stone shimmered a beautiful blue, like the sea. In the winter, it glowed like pure gold. The two sisters refused to share it. Each one wanted the stone for herself, and they argued all the time about who should have it. When Rachel's parents moved in between the two witches, they found themselves in the middle of a great argument.

Rachel was fed up with it. When the two witches were at their most angry, they made it rain. It had been raining now for two years.

And that wasn't all. Snatch and Grab shouted at each other through magic telephones made of giant sheep horns. They made smelly potions to upset each other, but these usually upset Rachel's mum more, especially when she wanted to hang the washing out. Sometimes they threw bolts of lightning at each other, which missed and landed in Rachel's back garden. In fact, Snatch and Grab were so busy arguing that they had forgotten all about the stone.

One day, in between rain storms, Rachel's mum and dad were sitting in the back garden and Rachel was playing in the front garden. Suddenly, she noticed something as bright as a pool of water, lying by the gate. It was the magic stone, and it was lovely! It shimmered as deep and as blue as a lake – and as Rachel looked at it, it spoke.

"They dropped me," said the stone, grumpily. "Can you believe that, eh?"

Rachel shook her head. The stone continued.

"They argue about me for years and years. Then they drop me and they don't even know that I'm gone. What a cheek!" It shone a bright leaf-green. "And think of all the trouble they have caused trying to get me – making bolts of fire, cooking up smells." The stone sighed. So did Rachel.

"They are rude," she said. "We should teach them a lesson."

"I don't think I can," the stone said in a sad voice. "What they don't realise is that they've used up nearly all my magic with their greedy quarrelling. I once belonged to a king of Egypt who wore me in his crown. Then I belonged to a mermaid who gave me to a brave and

handsome pirate. I am a very special magic stone. To think about the way all my power is being wasted by two silly old witches would break my heart, if I had one. The trouble is, if I stopped them now I would have no power left. All I would be is just a pretty stone."

As the stone said this, there was a terrific boom in the back garden. Rachel looked round and was just in time to see a huge cloud of yellow smoke rising up behind the house. She also saw a pair of long legs disappear over the top of the hedge into Snatch's garden. Rachel dashed through the house. When she reached the back garden she was horrified. On the two deck chairs, where her mother and father had been sitting, there were two huge plants. Snatch had tried to turn Grab into a giant plant, but the spell had gone wrong. She had turned Rachel's parents into plants, instead!

Rachel ran back to the stone and explained what had happened.

"You have to help me now," she cried.

"All right," said the stone. "I don't know that I want to be magic any more, anyway. It was fun when I belonged to the king of Egypt, but being used by silly witches to turn sensible people's parents into plants is quite another matter."

The stone began to glow, then it flashed until orange sparks flew. Then the stone hummed. It recited a spell very grandly, and the whole back garden shook.

"Keep no spells," declared the stone. "Let them be witches no more." There was a flash of light, a loud bang and the stone turned blue again.

Rachel could hear her parents chattering to one another in their deck chairs. She sighed with relief. But what of Snatch and Grab? Just as she was wondering what had become of them, Rachel saw the most remarkable thing. Grab came out of her house and walked toward Snatch, who had appeared at just the same time.

"How nice to see you," said Grab.

"How lovely to see you," replied Snatch.

"Do come in and have some tea, my dear," said Grab, and they both walked back into the house.

"I have your stone," Rachel called to them.

"Stone? What stone?" they both asked.

Rachel held up the stone, which was now a dull blue.

"Oh, that!" said the sisters, together. "Keep it!"

So Rachel kept the stone. It was no longer magic. It was no longer anything but a pretty stone. Snatch and Grab were no longer bad witches. Their argument was over and it never rained on Rachel's house again.

When Rachel was older she had the stone made into a brooch and always wore it on special occasions. It shone a beautiful blue in summer, and a rich gold in winter, and Rachel liked it better than all her other jewels. For it reminded her of how stupid arguments can be and, after all, who else has a brooch made of unicorn's horn and dragon's wing? Or, for that matter, one that once belonged to a pirate, an Egyptian king and two silly witches?

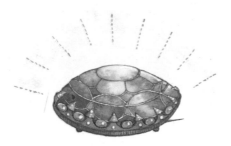

THE END